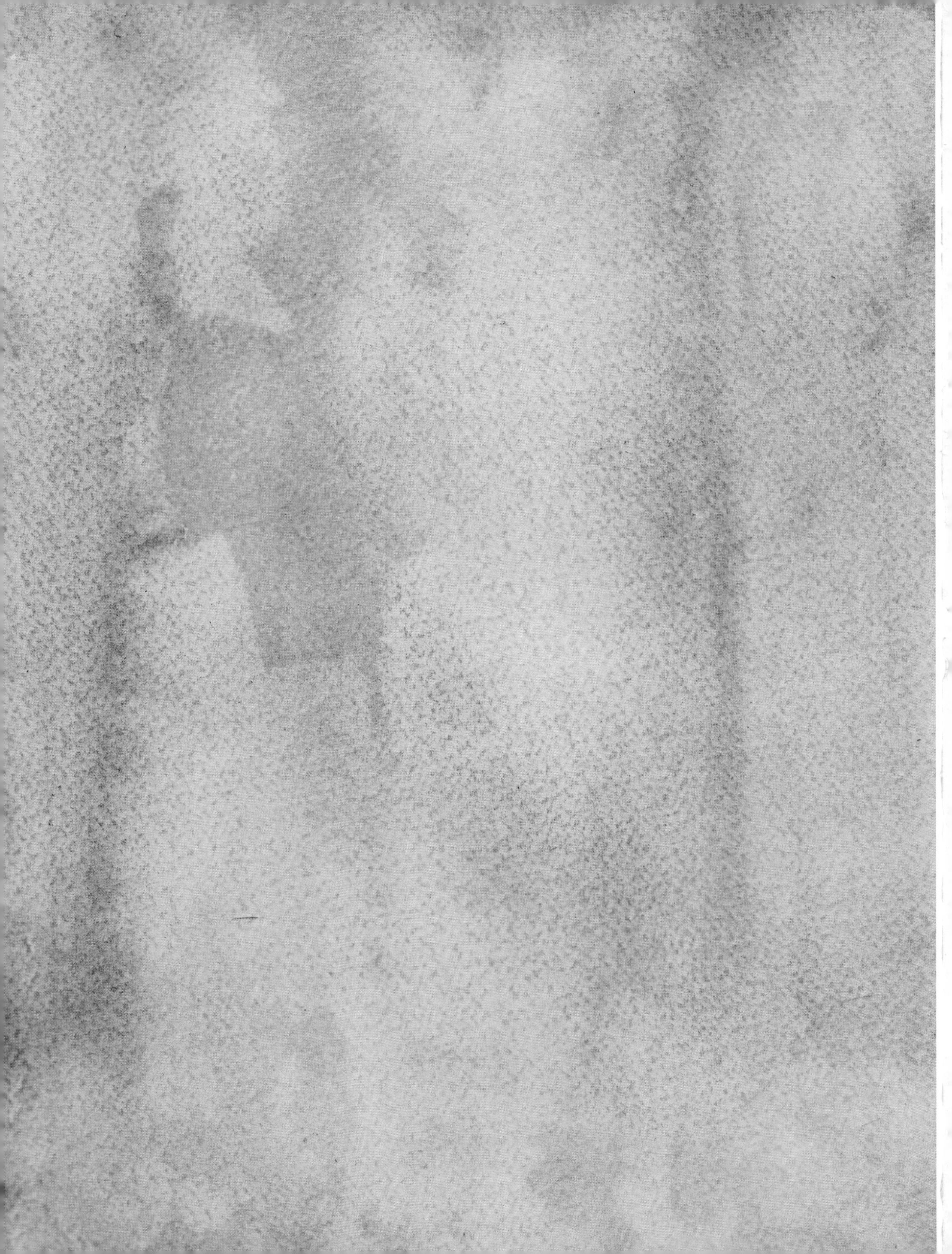

This book is dedicated to:

Arizona Equine Rescue Organization (AERO)
azequinerescue.org Soleil K. Dolce (Incident Lead)

AERO's Large Animal Rescue Volunteer Team (LAR)

Anonymous Donor

Superstition Search & Rescue (provided helmets, goggles, and walkie talkies)

Jeff Boatman & Gary Mercer of Airwest Helicopters

Central Arizona Mountain Rescue Team

Mark A. Eshenbaugh & Vickie L. Trask (owners of the horse)

John and Deb Fox of Large Animal Rescue Co.

Dr. Laura Harris (Landing Team Veterinarian)

Vinnie Konderick of the Phoenix Fire Department
(Landing Zone Incident Commander)

Dr. Julie Lucas of the Southwest Equine Medical & Surgical Center (Lift-off Team Veterinarian)

Jesse Robinson and Dave Bremson (Maricopa County Sheriff Search and Rescue Commanders)

Vaka Taimani (El Mirage Firefighter and LAR Instructor)

Colorado, the Flying Horse: A True Arizona Story

Happy Trails,
Suzanne M. Malpass

PRT0413A

Printed in the United States

ISBN-13: 9781620862766
ISBN-10: 162086276X

www.mascotbooks.com

COLORADO, THE FLYING HORSE

A True Arizona Story

Written by Suzanne M. Malpass

Illustrated by Trish Morgan

"Could you call 9-1-1 for me?" Mark blurted out as he rode up to the stranger. "We were caught in the river and our phones got junked," he continued as he jumped down off his stallion.

"O...kay," said the woman. She took a few steps back and dialed the numbers, while keeping an eye on the dripping-wet cowboy and his very large horse.

"A guy here needs help," said the woman. She approached warily, but did hand over her phone.

"What is your emergency, sir?"

"My wife and friends were swept away in the Gila." (pronounced HEE- la)

"How many others are we talking about, sir?"

"Vickie and two others. They were on horseback—the horses got dragged away, too."

"What's your location, sir?"

"We're somewhere near Eagle Mountain Road where Rainbow Road would cross it."

That morning, Mark, Vickie, and their dog, Annie Get Your Gun, arrived early at their friend Kirk's place. First, Mark trimmed the feet of the newest horse on the ranch. Next on his agenda was a twelve-mile trail ride with Vickie, Kirk, and another friend, Cindy, on some nearby state land.

The group drove about twenty minutes to Rainbow Valley and unloaded the animals and gear. As four horses, four riders, and one dog set off on that lovely morning in March, no one dreamed that a pleasant little trail ride might turn into a life-changing event.

After a few hours, the riders began to cross back over the Gila River to return to where they'd left the horse trailers. They were much further downstream from where they'd crossed before. The women were giggling and pulling their feet up to avoid getting their boots full of water.

Suddenly the current jammed them all together in swirling water seven feet deep. Before anyone could react, three people and three horses were carried away down the rampaging Gila.

For ninety-eight percent of the year, the Gila River is a dry riverbed so riders are accustomed to crossing it whenever and wherever they please. When the river is swollen and raging, its depth becomes very tricky to judge. Water at high speeds can scour away many feet of the sandy river bottom.

As everyone was pushed together, Mark wheeled his stallion, Cowpony, around and headed back the way they'd come. Cowpony had the advantage of being taller and stronger than the other horses. At one point he tripped on a submerged limb and the cowboy was fully dunked into the water. Luckily, he was able to pull himself back up onto the horse. Then he grabbed Annie off a partly submerged tree limb and pulled her across the saddle. The three struggled with each step, but made it through the driving current.

After reaching dry land, Mark dumped the water out of his boots. Then he, Cowpony, and Annie worked their way along the river to find help for the others.

Once the 9-1-1 call was completed, it took only seven minutes for a cruiser from the Maricopa County Sheriff's Office to arrive. The first responders assessed the situation, and then called in the Central Arizona Mountain Rescue Team. Once they arrived, the team concentrated on finding the missing people.

The raging current split around the biggest sandbar in the Gila and drove the terrified people toward the sides of the river. However, they couldn't get all the way to the banks because of the rocks and trees under the water. Had they reached the edge, steep banks would have presented yet another obstacle to safety.

Fortunately alongside the sandbar were several smaller sandbars, so Kirk was finally slowed down a bit. "Try to grab the trees! Try to grab the trees!" he yelled as first Cindy and then Vickie came into view. If the twenty-mile-an-hour current had swept the three beyond that sandbar, they would have had no chance to escape the angry river.

The mountain rescue team found them clinging desperately to branches sticking out of the water nearly two miles downstream from where they'd entered the river. One at a time, they were brought to safety by a team member tethered to a bright yellow rescue sled, which in turn was hooked to a power winch.

Finally all three, minus their cowboy hats, glasses, usable phones, and, in some cases, boots, were safe. Wrapped in a rescue blanket and looking beaten up, Vickie could not stop shivering or running her lower lip back and forth between her teeth. She worried about Colorado, the Navajo mustang she had been riding. "He swam back upstream to try to help me. Then he tread water near me for about twenty minutes," she said. "I kept trying to shoo him out of the river."

Meanwhile a tethered rescuer entered the water again, this time to remove or cut all equipment off the two horses that were caught in the partially submerged trees. Western saddles can weigh up to fifty pounds when dry. Their high profiles and the soaking wet horse blankets underneath added greatly to the drag on each animal.

Once freed of their burdens, the horses were able to climb out of the water. Then they fought their way through the thick tamarack and cottonwood growth along that section of the river to rejoin their riders.

Sometime later, the third missing horse was discovered on the highest ground in the river, part of the largest sandbar. Being a Navajo horse, Colorado had not been bred to look pretty in a show ring, but rather to be hearty and strong, with the brainpower to survive under difficult conditions.

Once the mustang was found, the sheriff's department landed its helicopter on the sandbar to try to remove his saddle. When the captain returned the saddle and blanket to Mark, he said, "I don't know who trained that horse, but he has personality plus. He wanted to get right on the copter with us. Most horses would not get anywhere near the prop wash of a helicopter."

Mark tipped his head to the left and grinned. "I trained Colorado," he said softly. Straightening up, he chuckled, "My daughter, Kyana, always claims she was the 'crash test dummy' during that training."

After doing all they could, the deputies suggested Vickie and Mark contact the Arizona Equine Rescue Organization (AERO) for help to try and recover their horse. AERO started its large-animal-rescue program after several horse-trailer accidents during which first responders either killed or injured horses, while trying to save them.

Some time later, the AERO team arrived, headed by Soleil (pronounced so-LAY), officially called the Incident Lead. They rejected the possibility of walking the horse out because of the high water.

In the previous months, record amounts of snow had fallen in the nearby mountains, while it rained on the desert below. The snowmelt caused overflowing lakes and rivers, which led the utility in charge to release countless gallons of water into the Gila. Even though the company, Salt River Project, would not be releasing any more water, their experts felt that the water around the sandbar would not recede for at least a month.

The AERO team also vetoed the idea of swimming the horse out. Soleil noted, "If we lost him there, he'd be in the wildest, most treacherous part of the river."

She and her team decided to do nothing in the short term because Colorado was safe on the two-acre sandbar and more rain was highly unlikely. The mustang had grass for forage, trees for shade, and, not surprisingly, an abundant supply of water.

A helicopter rescue was the only option left, but that would take lots of planning and scads of money.

Meanwhile a media storm had erupted and the helicopters from nearby television stations were following Colorado's every move. People at home were closely watching the horse's situation, too. Some even arrived late for work because they couldn't tear themselves away from the unfolding drama.

Reporters were besieging Vickie and Mark, as well as anyone connected with AERO. They even tracked Soleil down as she sat in a dentist chair having three cavities filled.

Some commentators offered wild speculation about the horse starving to death and other such nonsense, but AERO just kept working day after day to prepare for the rescue. Sometimes, when Mark came to check on his horse, he couldn't find him right away. "Where is he? Where is he? I can't see him anywhere!" Soleil remembers calming the cowboy down by saying, "Dude, it's okay—he's just lying down, sleeping under his favorite tree."

The heavy media coverage of Colorado's plight inspired an anonymous donor to come forth and pay for the entire rescue. This was an enormous relief for everyone involved.

While AERO was assembling an experienced large-animal-extraction team, they were also attempting to obtain a helicopter-rated sling from California. It would supplement the vertical-lift sling made of fire hose they had previously used, which was not certified for helicopter use.

Soleil drove to Glendale, Arizona to meet with Jeff, a pilot at Air West Helicopters. He was experienced in wild-animal extraction and planned to drop a net over Colorado and scoop him off the sandbar. "No, no, no, no," said Soleil. She explained that while it was sad if a wild elk or bear was hurt in transport, it was quite different if a treasured family pet was injured on national TV.

She added, "We AERO volunteers take training and then we teach police, fire fighters, vets; livestock and Bureau of Land Management personnel; reservation range managers, as well as search and rescue groups, how to safely manage horses in an emergency. Human instincts are often wrong."

"Our goal is that no people or animals are wounded or killed in large-animal-rescue attempts." The pilot agreed to AERO's plan and the date was set for early Tuesday morning, Colorado's fifth day on his island.

The night before the rescue attempt, Mark found it hard to sleep. He just kept worrying about the little mustang he'd raised from a colt that had always taken such good care of his kids. He'd allow himself a small smile, but then the seriousness of the situation would flood over him again. He knew if Colorado landed hard and broke a leg, he'd have to be put down.

Thankfully when the big day finally arrived, there were none of the strong winds which often buffet the area. Soleil and the rest of the takeoff team were helicoptered to the far end of the sandbar. They had brought treats, but didn't even need them because Colorado walked right up to them.

A veterinarian sedated the mustang and put cotton in his ears. Then the crew took an entire hour to carefully secure him in both slings. After being blindfolded, Colorado was hooked up for a trial lift just a few feet off the ground. The horse looked perfectly balanced and secure, so the team yelled and motioned, "Go! Go! Go! Go!" Even when he began to spin slowly, Colorado remained calm. His legs hung straight down and his tail flapped in the wind.

The takeoff volunteers were so carried away by the sight of a horse being airlifted off a sandbar, they forgot to tell the landing team that the mustang was on his way. Finally Soleil found her walkie talkie and reported in.

Approximately one-half mile away, the landing team was ready. Soon they could spot the flying horse, "moving around ten miles an hour, about a hundred feet below the Jet Bell Ranger and 100 feet above the ground," according to a television reporter. Onlookers, media types, and volunteers stared at a sight none had ever seen before.

Now came the pilot's most important job–setting the horse down gently. Nothing in his background of trail rides and ranch living could have prepared Colorado for a helicopter ride. An 850-pound panicked animal can be a major danger to itself and to anyone nearby. After the four-minute flight, the mustang hovered over the target area. Someone grabbed the rope hanging down from the headstall and guided the horse toward the landing spot. "Steady, Boy. Steady now. That's a good boy."

As his hoofs touched the ground, Colorado's legs buckled...but soon he was able to stand and support his own weight. The volunteers closed in around him as soon as possible so if there were any injury, the media couldn't see or film it. Mark spoke softly to Colorado to keep him calm.

As soon as the heavy slings were removed, the landing-scene vet checked Colorado's vital signs. "He's just fine. Everything's normal," she reported. "I cannot believe he came through that entire ordeal with only a little rub mark on his chest from one of the slings." Vickie and Mark hugged their horse, while thanking everyone who had helped.

Afterwards, Mark walked his groggy horse for a long time to wear off the tranquilizers. "They sure did nuke you, Boy," he kept saying. To a reporter, he explained his attachment to Colorado: "If you raise a horse from birth, the relationship is like that with your mom, your dad, your siblings, or your children. This little mustang is part of our family."

Thanks to the efforts of countless volunteers, Colorado is now back at home in Buckeye with his herd mates. When Soleil talks about the rescue, she says, "It was as if a rainbow had been dropped over that entire scenario. It absolutely could not have gone any better."

The End

A few words you may not know:

Buckeye, Arizona is the westernmost suburb of Phoenix.

Equine means of or relating to a horse, a donkey, or a mule.

The **Gila River** is a 649-mile-long tributary of the Colorado River. It flows through New Mexico and Arizona.

A **hand** equals four inches. It is used to measure the height of a horse. Colorado is 14.1 hands, 56.4 inches tall at the withers (shoulders). He weighs about 850 pounds. Cowpony is 16 hands, 64 inches at the withers, and weighs about 1150 pounds.

Mustangs were originally free-roaming horses of the North American West. They are descended from horses brought to the Americas by the Spanish.

A **stallion** is a male horse that has not been castrated.

Many thanks to my husband, Jeff Rogers, to my careful readers, Hollyann M. Brown, my son, Mark Rogers, and Jean Rubin, as well as to my stellar supporters: Heather Baker, Marsha Beck, Jody Clark, Evelyn and David Malpass, my twin sisters, Julia and Tina Malpass, Philip & Delores Malpass, Karen Smith, and, most especially, Anne Houser.

-Suzanne M. Malpass

Other books by Suzanne M. Malpass:

Stony's Tale: A True Tombstone Story

Rusty Tries Growing Up: A True Eastern Shore Story

A Lab's Tale